Connect with Mrigendra
Thank you very much for choosing this book.
You can also connect with me on Instagram,
https://www.instagram.com/i_mrigendrabharti.official
Thank You,
Mrigendra Bharti

Divine Union; The Love Story of Lord Ram and Maa Sita

Mrigendra Bharti

Published by Sellbrochure Vymish Entertainment, 2024.

This is a work of fiction. Similarities to real people, places, or events are entirely coincidental.

DIVINE UNION; THE LOVE STORY OF LORD RAM AND MAA SITA

First edition. June 14, 2024.

Copyright © 2024 Mrigendra Bharti.

ISBN: 979-8227614872

Written by Mrigendra Bharti.

Table of Contents

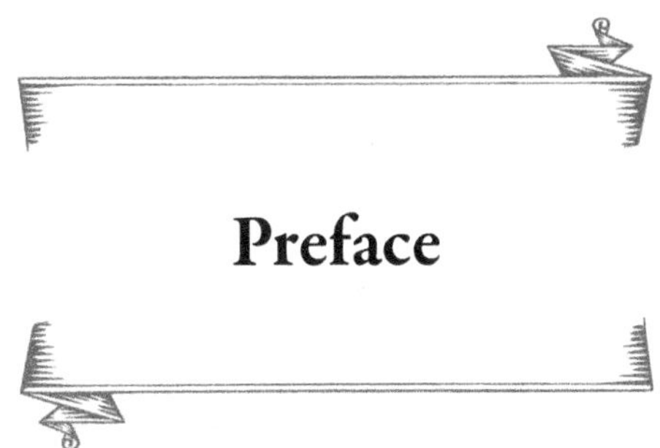

Preface

"DIVINE UNION: THE LOVE Story of Lord Ram and Maa Sita" is a tale that has inspired humanity for millennia with its profound messages of love, sacrifice, and devotion. This story is not only a part of sacred texts but also an integral component of India's cultural and spiritual heritage. The love story of Lord Ram and Maa Sita transcends the simple narrative of a prince and a princess, offering a glimpse into a relationship founded on principles, duty, and pure emotions.

This book aims to present their divine love story from a fresh perspective, exploring their meeting, marriage, exile, trials, and ultimate reunion. Through this narrative, we seek to delve into the depths of their characters, the challenges they faced, and the unwavering love and commitment that defined their relationship.

Each chapter of this book is meticulously crafted to bring forth the essence of their journey. From their first encounter in Mithila to the trials in the forest, from the epic battle in Lanka to the establishment of Ram Rajya, this book endeavors to capture the richness of their experiences and the lessons their story imparts.

In an age where the true meaning of love is often overshadowed by transient emotions, the story of Lord Ram and

Maa Sita stands as a beacon of eternal love and sacrifice. It is our hope that readers will find inspiration in their story and reflect on the values that made their union divine.

May this book serve as a bridge to connect you with the timeless wisdom and enduring love of Lord Ram and Maa Sita. As you embark on this journey through their lives, may you discover the profound beauty and spiritual depth that their story offers.

With reverence and love,
Mrigendra Bharti

Prologue

In the ancient land of Bharata, where rivers sang hymns of devotion and the mountains echoed the prayers of sages, there flourished a story that transcends time and space. It is a story of divine love, unwavering duty, and the eternal principles of dharma. This is the story of Lord Ram and Maa Sita, whose lives and love have been etched into the very soul of Indian culture.

Eons ago, in the kingdom of Ayodhya, there was born a prince named Ram, an embodiment of virtue and righteousness. Across the lands, in the kingdom of Mithila, the earth itself bore a divine gift, a princess named Sita, whose grace and purity were unmatched. Their destinies, intertwined by the threads of fate, set the stage for a love story that would endure for all eternity.

Their first meeting, like the merging of two celestial beings, was a moment of profound recognition and love. As Sita garlanded Ram during the swayamvar, their hearts united, promising to walk the path of life together. Yet, their journey was not to be one of ease and comfort. It was to be a path of trials, separation, and ultimate reunion, each step a testament to their unwavering love and commitment.

The fourteen years of exile in the forest tested their bond in ways unimaginable. Together, they faced the harshness of the wilderness, the scheming of demons, and the pain of separation. When Sita was abducted by the demon king Ravana, it was not just an act of evil but a test of their love's strength. Ram's tireless search for Sita, aided by his loyal brother Laxman and the devoted Hanuman, symbolized the power of love and devotion overcoming the greatest of obstacles.

The climactic battle in Lanka was not just a fight between good and evil but a declaration of love's triumph over darkness.

Sita's agni pariksha, her trial by fire, symbolized purity and the ultimate sacrifice. Their return to Ayodhya and the establishment of Ram Rajya, the ideal kingdom, marked the fulfillment of their divine mission.

In a world often overshadowed by fleeting emotions and transient relationships, the love story of Ram and Sita stands as a beacon of eternal truth and purity. Their story, filled with trials and triumphs, teaches us the timeless values of love, duty, and righteousness.

As you turn the pages of this book, "Divine Union: The Love Story of Lord Ram and Maa Sita," may you be transported to an era where divine principles guided human lives, and may you find inspiration in their enduring love. This prologue is but a doorway to the profound journey of Ram and Sita, a journey that will leave an indelible mark on your heart and soul.

With reverence and hope,
Mrigendra Bharti

Acknowledgments

Writing "Divine Union: The Love Story of Lord Ram and Maa Sita" has been a deeply enriching and fulfilling journey. This book is a labor of love and devotion, inspired by the timeless tale of Lord Ram and Maa Sita.

I extend my heartfelt gratitude to the countless storytellers, ancient texts, and cultural traditions that have kept this divine story alive through the ages. The wisdom and inspiration drawn from these sources have been invaluable in crafting this narrative.

This book is a tribute to the enduring power of love, sacrifice, and devotion. It is my sincere hope that it resonates with readers and brings them closer to the profound beauty and spiritual depth of Lord Ram and Maa Sita's love story.

Thank you for embarking on this journey with me.

With deep appreciation,

Mrigendra Bharti

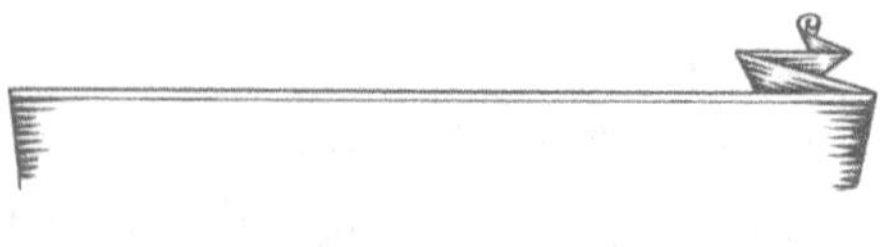

Introduction

"DIVINE UNION: THE LOVE Story of Lord Ram and Maa Sita" is more than just a tale of romance; it is an exploration of the profound principles of dharma, devotion, and the eternal bond that transcends time and space. This book delves into the epic journey of Lord Ram and Maa Sita, whose lives and love have become the cornerstone of Indian culture and spirituality.

From their auspicious births to their eventual reunion, the story of Ram and Sita is filled with moments that reflect the ideals of virtue, courage, and unwavering commitment. As we traverse through the chapters of this book, we will witness their journey through various stages of life, each filled with its own set of challenges and triumphs.

The first chapter introduces us to the divine origins of Ram and Sita, setting the stage for their eventual meeting. Their first encounter, filled with a profound sense of recognition and love, marks the beginning of a relationship that would endure countless trials. The second chapter explores their wedding, a grand celebration of their union and the beginning of their shared journey.

The third chapter takes us through their years of exile, where their love and devotion are put to the test in the harshness of the wilderness. Despite the adversities they face, their bond only grows stronger. The fourth chapter recounts the epic battle in Lanka, symbolizing the triumph of good over evil and the power of love to overcome even the darkest of times.

The final chapter reflects on the legacy of Ram and Sita, their return to Ayodhya, and the establishment of Ram Rajya, an ideal kingdom based on principles of justice and compassion. Their story continues to inspire millions, offering timeless lessons on the nature of true love, sacrifice, and the fulfillment of one's duties.

In writing this book, I have endeavored to capture the essence of their divine love story, presenting it in a way that resonates with contemporary readers while staying true to its ancient roots. Each chapter is crafted to bring forth the richness of their experiences, the depth of their characters, and the spiritual significance of their journey.

"Divine Union: The Love Story of Lord Ram and Maa Sita" invites you to immerse yourself in the timeless tale of two souls destined to be together, whose love and devotion continue to inspire and uplift humanity. As you read through these pages, may you find not only a beautiful love story but also the wisdom and strength to embrace the values that Ram and Sita embody.

With heartfelt reverence,

Mrigendra Bharti

Founder of Sellbrochure Vymish Entertainment

Chapter 1: Introduction

Part 1: Introduction of Lord Ram and Maa Sita

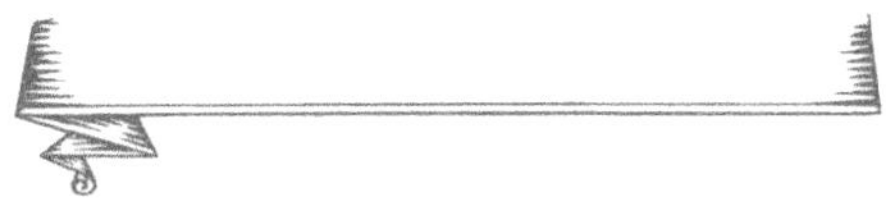

IN THE ANCIENT LAND of Bharata, where the majestic Ganges flowed and the Himalayas stood as silent sentinels, the tales of divine beings and celestial occurrences were woven into the very fabric of life. Among these tales, none is more revered or enduring than the story of Lord Ram and Maa Sita, the epitome of dharma and devotion.

Lord Ram, the seventh incarnation of Lord Vishnu, was born in the kingdom of Ayodhya, a prosperous and pious realm ruled by King Dasharatha of the Ikshvaku dynasty. Ayodhya, with its grand palaces, bustling markets, and serene temples, was a city where dharma, the righteous path, was the guiding principle of life. The people of Ayodhya revered their king, who was known for his justice, valor, and devotion to the gods.

In this blessed city, Queen Kaushalya, the principal queen of King Dasharatha, gave birth to a son who would change the course of history. Named Ram, this child was no ordinary prince. From a young age, he exhibited qualities that set him apart. His compassion, sense of justice, and unwavering devotion to truth earned him the love and admiration of all who knew him. Ram's presence brought a sense of peace and righteousness wherever he went, embodying the virtues that his kingdom cherished.

Ram's education was entrusted to the wise sage Vashishta, who imparted to him not only the knowledge of the Vedas and other sacred texts but also the principles of governance, warfare, and ethics. Under Vashishta's tutelage, Ram grew into a warrior of unparalleled skill and a leader of exceptional wisdom. His physical prowess was matched only by his humility and respect for all living beings, making him the ideal prince and the future king that Ayodhya awaited with bated breath.

Meanwhile, in the kingdom of Mithila, another story of divine origin was unfolding. Mithila, ruled by the wise and just King Janaka, was a land of great spiritual significance. King Janaka, known for his deep philosophical insights and adherence to dharma, was a ruler whose fame spread far and wide. His kingdom was

Part 2: Devotion and Virtues

IN THE KINGDOM OF MITHILA, the divine presence of Maa Sita graced the land with her ethereal beauty and unwavering devotion. Born from the earth itself, she was no ordinary princess but a symbol of purity, grace, and virtue. From her infancy, Sita displayed qualities that marked her as someone special. Her kindness, compassion, and devotion to her father King Janaka endeared her to all who knew her.

Under the loving guidance of her father and the wise counsel of the sages in Mithila, Sita grew into a paragon of virtue and righteousness. She immersed herself in the study of scriptures, the arts, and the duties befitting a princess of her stature. Her unwavering devotion to Lord Vishnu, whom she regarded as her eternal consort, served as a beacon of light in the kingdom, inspiring others to walk the path of righteousness.

As Sita blossomed into womanhood, her fame spread far and wide, drawing suitors from distant lands who sought her hand in marriage. Yet, Sita remained steadfast in her devotion to Lord Vishnu, awaiting the arrival of the one destined to be her husband. Her purity of heart and steadfastness in dharma captured the attention of all, including the gods in heaven who watched her with awe and reverence.

Meanwhile, in the kingdom of Ayodhya, the news of King Dasharatha's desire to crown Lord Ram as his heir spread like wildfire. The prospect of Ram's ascension to the throne filled the hearts of the people with joy and anticipation. Ram's virtues, his unwavering commitment to dharma, and his compassion for all living beings endeared him to the citizens of Ayodhya, who eagerly awaited the day when he would lead them as their king.

As fate would have it, the divine union of Lord Ram and Maa Sita was not a mere coincidence but a cosmic arrangement orchestrated by the gods themselves. Their love story, which would transcend the boundaries of time and space, was about to unfold in ways that would captivate the hearts and minds of generations to come.

Part 3: Divine Destinies

IN THE CELESTIAL REALMS, where the gods and goddesses resided, whispers of a divine union between Lord Ram and Maa Sita echoed through the cosmos. For ages, the cosmic balance had been meticulously maintained by the divine orchestrations of Lord Vishnu, the preserver of the universe. And now, the time had come for one of the most significant chapters in the cosmic drama to unfold—the union of two divine souls, destined to bring about the dawning of a new era.

The divine destinies of Lord Ram and Maa Sita were intricately intertwined since time immemorial. As incarnations of the divine, their union was not a matter of chance but a preordained event that would shape the course of history and inspire countless souls for generations to come. Each step they took, each trial they faced, was part of a grand cosmic plan that would ultimately lead them to each other's embrace.

In the celestial abode of Lord Vishnu, the gods and goddesses eagerly awaited the unfolding of this divine drama. Brahma, the creator, with his infinite wisdom, had foreseen the events that would transpire and had woven the threads of fate with meticulous care. Shiva, the destroyer, in his eternal meditation, recognized the significance of this union in the grand tapestry of existence. And Devi Lakshmi, the goddess of wealth and fortune, showered her blessings upon the divine couple, ensuring that their love would endure all trials and tribulations.

As Lord Ram embarked on his journey to Mithila with his beloved brother Laxman and the sage Vishwamitra, the celestial beings rejoiced, knowing that the moment of their union was drawing near. In the sacred groves of Mithila, where the swayamvar of Maa Sita was to take place, the atmosphere was charged with anticipation and excitement. Kings and princes from far and wide gathered to compete for the hand of the divine princess, unaware of the cosmic significance of the event unfolding before them.

For Maa Sita, the swayamvar was not just a ceremony but a sacred opportunity to fulfill her divine destiny. As she adorned herself with exquisite ornaments and prepared to choose her consort, her heart was filled with the presence of Lord Ram, whose image was etched in her mind since time immemorial. With every breath, she prayed for the fulfillment of her divine purpose, knowing that her beloved would soon arrive to claim her as his own.

And then, as if guided by unseen forces, Lord Ram entered the swayamvar hall, his presence illuminating the space with divine radiance. With a calm and composed demeanor, he approached the bow of Lord Shiva, which stood as a symbol of strength and valor. With effortless ease, he lifted the mighty bow and strung it with a single arrow, a feat that no mortal had ever achieved before.

As the assembled kings and princes looked on in awe, Maa Sita's heart leaped with joy, for she knew that the moment she had been waiting for had finally arrived. With eyes filled with love and reverence, she garlanded Lord Ram, sealing their union in the presence of the gods and goddesses who watched over them. And in that sacred moment, the heavens resounded with celestial music, heralding the beginning of a new era—the era of divine love and union.

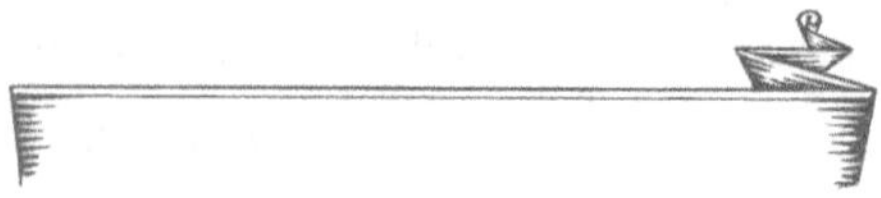

Part 4: Setting the Stage

WITH THE DIVINE UNION of Lord Ram and Maa Sita, the stage was set for a saga that would captivate the hearts and minds of all who heard it. In the celestial realms, the gods and goddesses rejoiced, showering their blessings upon the divine couple as they embarked on their journey together. But little did they know that the path ahead would be fraught with trials and tribulations, testing the strength of their love and devotion to the fullest.

In the kingdom of Ayodhya, preparations were underway for the grand wedding ceremony of Lord Ram and Maa Sita. The city bustled with activity as artisans crafted exquisite decorations, musicians rehearsed melodious tunes, and priests chanted sacred hymns in anticipation of the auspicious occasion. The air was filled with an aura of joy and celebration, as the citizens of Ayodhya eagerly awaited the arrival of their beloved prince and his divine bride.

Meanwhile, in the heavenly abode of Lord Vishnu, discussions were underway among the gods and goddesses about the role they would play in the unfolding drama on Earth. Brahma, with his infinite wisdom, laid out the cosmic plan, while Shiva, with his unwavering resolve, vowed to protect the divine couple from any harm that may befall them. Devi

Lakshmi, in her infinite grace, showered her blessings upon the kingdom of Ayodhya, ensuring that prosperity and happiness would reign supreme.

As the wedding day dawned, the sun rose with renewed brilliance, casting its golden rays upon the city of Ayodhya. The streets were lined with flowers and garlands, and the sound of bells and conch shells filled the air, heralding the auspicious occasion. Lord Ram, resplendent in his royal attire, rode atop a magnificent chariot, accompanied by his brothers, friends, and well-wishers, as they made their way to Mithila to claim his bride.

In Mithila, Maa Sita, adorned in the finest silks and jewels, awaited the arrival of her beloved with bated breath. Her heart swelled with anticipation as she prepared to embark on a new journey with the man she loved more than life itself. Surrounded by her family and friends, she offered prayers to the gods for the happiness and prosperity of Ayodhya and for the success of her union with Lord Ram.

And as Lord Ram and his entourage arrived in Mithila, the heavens themselves seemed to rejoice, showering the earth with fragrant flowers and sweet nectar. The divine couple, their eyes alight with love and devotion, exchanged garlands amidst the cheers and blessings of the assembled throng, sealing their union for eternity.

With their wedding ceremony complete, Lord Ram and Maa Sita set out for Ayodhya, their hearts filled with joy and anticipation for the life that lay ahead. Little did they know that their journey together would be marked by trials and tribulations that would test the very fabric of their love and devotion. But for now, in this moment of divine union, all was right with the world, and nothing could mar the happiness and bliss that enveloped them.

Chapter 2: Meeting and Marriage

Part 1: Swayamvar ka Ayojan

IN THE GRAND KINGDOM of Mithila, the auspicious occasion of Maa Sita's swayamvar was a spectacle unlike any other. The city was adorned with vibrant decorations, and the air was filled with the sweet fragrance of flowers. Kings, princes, and nobles from far and wide had gathered to compete for the hand of the divine princess, each hoping to win her favor and claim her as their bride.

The swayamvar ceremony was a time-honored tradition in Mithila, where the princess had the liberty to choose her own consort from among the assembled suitors. The stakes were high, and the competition fierce, as each contender sought to prove his worthiness through feats of strength, skill, and valor.

As the appointed day of the swayamvar dawned, the kingdom of Mithila bustled with activity. The streets were lined with spectators eager to catch a glimpse of the divine princess and her illustrious suitors. The palace grounds, adorned with intricate tapestries and ornate decorations, bore witness to the grandeur of the occasion.

Inside the palace, King Janaka, accompanied by his illustrious guests, presided over the proceedings with regal grace and dignity. The atmosphere was charged with anticipation as the assembled suitors awaited their turn to showcase their talents and vie for the hand of the princess.

Among the contenders was Lord Ram, the prince of Ayodhya, whose reputation for valor and righteousness preceded him. Accompanied by his beloved brother Laxman and the sage Vishwamitra, Lord Ram exuded an aura of divine radiance that set him apart from the other suitors. His presence drew the admiration of all who beheld him, and whispers of his divine lineage spread through the crowd like wildfire.

As the ceremony commenced, each suitor was called forth to demonstrate his prowess in a series of challenges designed to test his worthiness. Some attempted to lift the mighty bow of Lord Shiva, while others engaged in feats of archery, swordsmanship, and intellectual debate.

Amidst the spectacle, Lord Ram stood poised and composed, his gaze fixed upon the divine princess whose image had captured his heart. With each passing moment, his longing to win her hand grew stronger, fueled by the deep sense of connection he felt with her soul.

And then, as the sun reached its zenith and the tension reached its peak, Maa Sita made her grand entrance, her beauty illuminating the hall like a thousand suns. Dressed in resplendent attire, adorned with jewels that sparkled like stars in the night sky, she moved with grace and poise befitting a princess of divine lineage.

As the suitors looked on in awe, Maa Sita approached the bow of Lord Shiva, her eyes alight with determination and resolve. With a steady hand, she lifted the bow with ease, a feat that none had dared to attempt before. And in that moment, the heavens themselves seemed to rejoice, showering the earth with blessings and divine music.

As the ceremony drew to a close, King Janaka addressed the assembled crowd, declaring Maa Sita's swayamvar a resounding success. But little did he know that the most significant event of the day was yet to come—a moment that would change the course of history and unite two divine souls in eternal love.

Part 2: The Divine Encounter

WITH THE SWAYAMVAR ceremony concluded, the atmosphere in the palace of Mithila was charged with anticipation as the guests awaited the next phase of the proceedings. Among them, Lord Ram, accompanied by his loyal brother Laxman and the sage Vishwamitra, stood with bated breath, his heart filled with longing for the divine princess whose image had captured his soul.

Meanwhile, Maa Sita, resplendent in her divine beauty, retired to her chambers, her mind abuzz with thoughts of the suitor who had captured her heart. Despite the dazzling array of suitors who had vied for her hand, her thoughts kept returning to the prince from Ayodhya, whose presence had left an indelible mark upon her soul.

As if guided by unseen forces, Lord Ram found himself drawn to Maa Sita's chambers, his heart racing with anticipation at the prospect of beholding her once more. With each step, his longing grew stronger, fueled by the deep sense of connection he felt with her across the vast expanse of space and time.

Upon reaching Maa Sita's chambers, Lord Ram was greeted by a scene of ethereal beauty, as the divine princess sat in quiet contemplation amidst the soft glow of candlelight. Her eyes, like pools of liquid moonlight, met his own, and in that instant, a silent understanding passed between them—an unspoken recognition of the divine bond that united their souls.

With trembling hands and a heart full of reverence, Lord Ram approached Maa Sita, his every movement infused with the grace and dignity befitting a prince of his stature. As he knelt before her, he spoke words of admiration and respect, expressing his deepest longing to be united with her for all eternity.

Moved by his sincerity and devotion, Maa Sita's heart swelled with love and compassion, as she gazed upon the prince from Ayodhya with eyes filled with tenderness and affection. In that sacred moment, the barriers of time and space seemed to dissolve, and their souls merged in a divine embrace that transcended the limitations of mortal existence.

As they sat in quiet communion, the world outside faded into insignificance, as they became lost in the timeless depths of each other's presence. For in that fleeting moment of divine encounter, Lord Ram and Maa Sita found solace in the knowledge that their love was ordained by the heavens and destined to endure for all eternity.

And as the night wore on and the stars danced in the heavens, Lord Ram and Maa Sita remained locked in a silent embrace, their hearts intertwined in a bond of love that would withstand the test of time and conquer all obstacles in its path. For theirs was not just a love story, but a divine union that would shape the destiny of the cosmos itself.

Part 3: The Challenge of Worthiness

IN THE WAKE OF THE divine encounter between Lord Ram and Maa Sita, the atmosphere in the palace of Mithila was fraught with tension and anticipation. As the suitors who had failed to win the hand of the princess licked their wounds and nursed their bruised egos, whispers of jealousy and resentment spread through the crowd like wildfire.

Among the assembled guests, King Janaka, ever the wise and discerning ruler, observed the proceedings with a keen eye, his thoughts shrouded in contemplation as he pondered the fate of his beloved daughter. For he knew that the task of choosing a worthy consort for Maa Sita was not one to be taken lightly, and that the responsibility rested upon his shoulders alone.

Meanwhile, Lord Ram, his heart filled with a sense of purpose and determination, resolved to prove himself worthy of Maa Sita's hand in marriage. With the sage Vishwamitra by his side, he prepared to face the challenges that lay ahead, knowing that the path to true love was fraught with obstacles and trials.

As the sun rose on the following day, King Janaka summoned the assembled suitors to the grand arena, where a series of tests awaited them. The challenges were designed to test not only their physical prowess but also their intellect, courage, and moral character—the qualities that King Janaka deemed essential in a worthy consort for his daughter.

One by one, the suitors stepped forward to face the trials, each determined to prove his worthiness in the eyes of the princess and her esteemed father. Some engaged in feats of strength and skill, while others participated in intellectual debates and philosophical discourses, each hoping to catch Maa Sita's eye and win her favor.

Amidst the spectacle, Lord Ram stood poised and composed, his every movement infused with grace and dignity. With each trial he faced, he demonstrated not only his physical prowess but also his unwavering commitment to dharma and righteousness, earning the admiration and respect of all who beheld him.

But it was not only Lord Ram who impressed the assembled guests with his valor and virtue. Maa Sita, ever the discerning judge of character, observed the proceedings with keen interest, her heart stirred by the courage and nobility displayed by the prince from Ayodhya.

And as the challenges drew to a close and the sun dipped below the horizon, King Janaka addressed the crowd, declaring Lord Ram the victor of the trials and the chosen consort for his beloved daughter. With tears of joy and gratitude in her eyes, Maa Sita approached Lord Ram, her heart overflowing with love and devotion for the prince who had captured her soul.

In that sacred moment, amidst the cheers and blessings of the assembled throng, Lord Ram and Maa Sita sealed their union with a vow of eternal love and devotion, setting the stage for a love story that would endure for all eternity.

Part 4: The Union of Hearts

WITH THE TRIALS OF worthiness concluded and Lord Ram declared the chosen consort for Maa Sita, the kingdom of Mithila erupted in jubilation and celebration. The air was filled with the sound of music and laughter as the people rejoiced in the union of two divine souls whose love had conquered all obstacles.

In the grand palace of Mithila, preparations were underway for the sacred wedding ceremony that would unite Lord Ram and Maa Sita in the bonds of holy matrimony. The palace grounds were adorned with fragrant flowers and colorful decorations, while priests chanted sacred hymns and performed elaborate rituals to invoke the blessings of the gods upon the divine couple.

As the auspicious hour approached, Lord Ram and Maa Sita, dressed in resplendent attire befitting their divine status, made their way to the wedding pavilion, their hearts brimming with love and devotion for each other. Surrounded by their families, friends, and well-wishers, they took their places beneath the sacred canopy, ready to embark on a journey of love and companionship that would span the ages.

As the priests chanted Vedic hymns and performed the sacred rites, Lord Ram and Maa Sita exchanged vows of eternal love and fidelity, pledging to stand by each other through all the trials and tribulations that life may bring. With each sacred mantra, their bond grew stronger, as the gods themselves bore witness to the union of two souls destined to be together for all eternity.

And then, as the final blessings were bestowed and the sacred fire was lit, Lord Ram and Maa Sita took the seven steps around the holy fire, symbolizing their commitment to each other and the journey they would undertake together as husband and wife. With each step, they prayed for love, prosperity, and happiness, knowing that their union was blessed by the gods themselves.

As the wedding ceremony drew to a close and the guests offered their heartfelt congratulations to the newlyweds, the heavens themselves seemed to rejoice, showering the earth with blessings and divine light. For in that sacred moment, the union of Lord Ram and Maa Sita heralded the dawn of a new era—a golden age of love, righteousness, and divine grace that would illuminate the world for generations to come.

And so, amidst the cheers and blessings of the assembled throng, Lord Ram and Maa Sita embarked on their journey together, their hearts united in love and devotion, their souls bound by the eternal bonds of divine destiny. For theirs was not just a marriage of two individuals, but a union of two divine souls whose love would transcend the boundaries of time and space, inspiring countless generations with its purity and devotion.

Chapter 3: The Exile Begins

Part 1: Departure from Ayodhya

AS THE GOLDEN RAYS of dawn illuminated the city of Ayodhya, casting a warm glow upon its majestic palaces and bustling streets, a sense of anticipation hung in the air. For on this auspicious day, the kingdom would bear witness to the departure of its beloved prince, Lord Ram, on a journey that would alter the course of history.

In the royal palace, preparations were underway for the departure ceremony, as servants bustled about, ensuring that every detail was attended to with the utmost care and precision. The atmosphere was tinged with both sorrow and reverence, as the citizens of Ayodhya gathered to bid farewell to their beloved prince, whose selfless sacrifice would forever be etched in the annals of history.

Amidst the throng of well-wishers, Lord Ram stood with a calm and composed demeanor, his noble bearing and unwavering resolve a testament to his character and strength of will. Beside him stood his devoted wife, Maa Sita, radiant with grace and beauty, her eyes filled with love and devotion for her beloved husband.

As the departure ceremony commenced, King Dasharatha, his heart heavy with sorrow yet filled with pride, addressed the assembled crowd, his voice resonating with authority and reverence. With tears in his eyes, he spoke of Lord Ram's virtues and noble qualities, praising his son's unwavering commitment to dharma and righteousness.

With a heavy heart, King Dasharatha then turned to Lord Ram and beseeched him to fulfill his duty as a prince and uphold the honor of the Ikshvaku dynasty. Lord Ram, ever the epitome of humility and obedience, bowed before his father and pledged to honor his wishes, even at the cost of his own happiness and well-being.

As the departure ceremony drew to a close, Lord Ram, Maa Sita, and his loyal brother Laxman made their way to the chariot that awaited them, their hearts heavy with the knowledge of the trials and tribulations that lay ahead. With one last lingering look at the city of Ayodhya, their home and birthplace, they set forth on their journey into the unknown, their destiny guided by the hands of fate.

As they journeyed through the vast expanse of the kingdom, the landscape gradually transformed from the lush greenery of Ayodhya to the rugged terrain of the wilderness. Yet, amidst the challenges and hardships they encountered along the way, Lord Ram remained steadfast in his resolve, his unwavering faith in the righteousness of his path serving as a beacon of hope and inspiration for all who accompanied him.

And so, as the sun began to set on the horizon, casting long shadows across the land, Lord Ram, Maa Sita, and Laxman continued on their journey into the unknown, their hearts filled with courage and determination, their spirits unyielding in the face of adversity. For theirs was a journey of self-discovery and enlightenment, a quest to fulfill their divine destiny and uphold the principles of righteousness and dharma for all eternity.

Part 2: Trials of the Wilderness

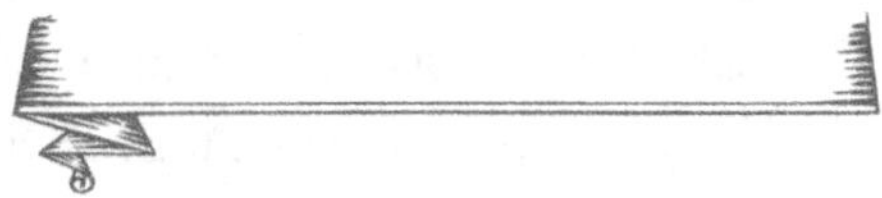

AS LORD RAM, MAA SITA, and Laxman ventured deeper into the wilderness, the challenges they faced grew more formidable with each passing day. The once-familiar sights and sounds of the kingdom of Ayodhya were replaced by the harsh realities of the untamed wilderness, where danger lurked at every turn and survival was a constant struggle.

With each step they took, they encountered new obstacles and adversaries that tested their courage, resilience, and faith in the divine. From ferocious beasts to treacherous terrain, every aspect of the wilderness seemed determined to thwart their progress and derail their quest.

Yet, amidst the trials and tribulations they faced, Lord Ram remained steadfast in his devotion to dharma and righteousness, his unwavering faith in the divine guiding him through the darkest of times. With his trusty bow and arrow by his side, he fearlessly confronted every challenge that came his way, his valor and skill unmatched by any mortal foe.

Maa Sita, ever the embodiment of grace and resilience, stood by Lord Ram's side with unwavering devotion, her unwavering faith in her husband's ability to overcome any obstacle serving as a source of strength and inspiration. Despite the hardships they faced, her love for Lord Ram remained unshakable, a beacon of light in the darkest of nights.

And then there was Laxman, the loyal brother and devoted companion, whose unwavering dedication to Lord Ram and Maa Sita knew no bounds. With his unmatched strength and courage, he stood as a stalwart protector, shielding them from harm and ensuring their safety at every turn.

Together, they traversed through dense forests, crossed raging rivers, and scaled towering mountains, each step bringing them closer to their ultimate destination. Along the way, they encountered sages and ascetics who imparted invaluable wisdom and guidance, helping them navigate the complexities of the wilderness and overcome the trials that lay ahead.

Yet, amidst the hardships and challenges they faced, there were moments of solace and serenity, where the beauty of the natural world filled their hearts with wonder and awe. In the tranquil stillness of the forest, amidst the rustling of leaves and the gentle whisper of the wind, they found solace in the embrace of nature, a reminder of the divine presence that surrounded them at all times.

And so, as they journeyed deeper into the heart of the wilderness, their spirits undaunted by the trials they faced, Lord Ram, Maa Sita, and Laxman remained united in their quest to fulfill their divine destiny. For theirs was not merely a journey of survival, but a pilgrimage of the soul—a quest for enlightenment and self-discovery that would ultimately lead them to the realization of their true purpose in life.

Part 3: Encounters with Divine Beings

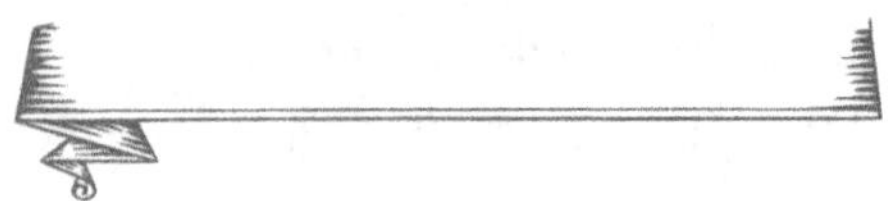

AS LORD RAM, MAA SITA, and Laxman continued their journey through the wilderness, they encountered a myriad of divine beings whose presence served as both guidance and challenge along their path.

Their first encounter came in the form of the sage Agastya, a revered ascetic whose wisdom and knowledge of the scriptures were unmatched. Recognizing Lord Ram's divine nature, Agastya imparted invaluable teachings and blessings upon the trio, guiding them on the path of righteousness and enlightenment.

Next, they encountered the mystical bird Jatayu, whose noble sacrifice in defense of Maa Sita would forever be etched in the annals of history. Despite his valiant efforts to protect her from harm, Jatayu fell prey to the demon king Ravana, leaving Lord Ram and his companions grief-stricken yet undeterred in their quest.

Their journey also brought them into contact with the monkey king Sugriva, whose friendship and loyalty would prove instrumental in their quest to rescue Maa Sita from the clutches of Ravana. With Sugriva's assistance, Lord Ram forged an alliance with the monkey army, paving the way for their eventual victory over the forces of darkness.

But perhaps their most fateful encounter came in the form of Hanuman, the devoted disciple of Lord Ram whose unwavering devotion and boundless courage would forever be remembered in the annals of history. With his unmatched strength and intelligence, Hanuman played a pivotal role in the search for Maa Sita, traversing great distances and overcoming seemingly insurmountable obstacles to bring news of her whereabouts to Lord Ram.

Each encounter with these divine beings served to strengthen Lord Ram's resolve and deepen his understanding of his true purpose in life. Through their guidance and support, he learned the importance of compassion, humility, and devotion in the face of adversity, qualities that would ultimately lead him to victory over the forces of darkness and the restoration of dharma to the world.

And so, as Lord Ram, Maa Sita, and Laxman journeyed onward, their hearts filled with gratitude for the divine beings who had crossed their path, they remained steadfast in their quest to fulfill their divine destiny and uphold the principles of righteousness and dharma for all eternity.

Part 4: The Battle of Good and Evil

AS LORD RAM, MAA SITA, and Laxman continued their journey, they found themselves drawn inexorably into the heart of darkness, where the forces of evil lay in wait. Led by the demon king Ravana, whose thirst for power and conquest knew no bounds, these malevolent beings sought to plunge the world into chaos and despair, threatening to unravel the very fabric of existence.

With his vast armies and formidable powers, Ravana posed a formidable challenge to Lord Ram and his companions, whose unwavering commitment to righteousness and dharma stood in stark contrast to the forces of darkness that sought to destroy them. Yet, despite the odds stacked against them, they remained undaunted in their resolve to confront evil and restore peace to the world.

The battle that ensued was nothing short of epic, a clash of titanic forces that shook the very foundations of the earth. From the battlefield of Lanka to the gates of heaven itself, Lord Ram and his allies fought with courage and determination, their valor and righteousness serving as a beacon of hope for all who stood against the forces of darkness.

In the midst of the chaos and carnage, Maa Sita remained steadfast in her faith and devotion to Lord Ram, her unwavering love serving as a source of strength and inspiration for him in the darkest of times. Though she was held captive by Ravana, her spirit remained unbroken, her resolve unwavering as she awaited the moment when her beloved would come to rescue her from the clutches of evil.

And come he did, with the fury of a thousand suns and the righteousness of a thousand saints. With his divine bow and arrow in hand, Lord Ram unleashed a torrent of destruction upon the forces of darkness, his every movement guided by the hand of fate and the blessings of the gods themselves. And as the battle raged on, the heavens themselves seemed to tremble with the ferocity of his wrath, as the forces of good and evil clashed in a final, cataclysmic showdown.

In the end, it was Lord Ram's unwavering commitment to righteousness and dharma that proved to be his greatest weapon against the forces of darkness. With a single stroke of his arrow, he vanquished Ravana and his armies, restoring peace and order to the world and securing victory for the forces of good.

And as the dust settled and the echoes of battle faded into the distance, Lord Ram, Maa Sita, and Laxman emerged triumphant, their hearts filled with gratitude for the divine beings who had guided and protected them along their journey. For theirs was not just a victory over the forces of darkness, but a triumph of the human spirit—a testament to the power of love, courage, and righteousness to overcome even the greatest of challenges.

Chapter 4: Return to Ayodhya

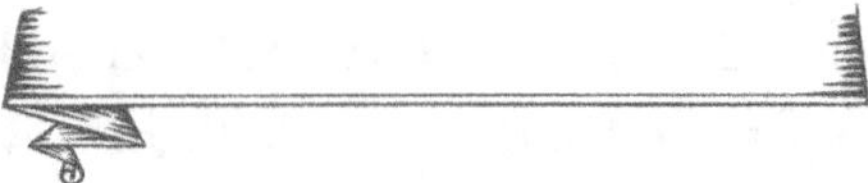

Part 1: Triumph and Reunion

WITH THE FORCES OF darkness vanquished and peace restored to the world, Lord Ram, Maa Sita, and Laxman embarked on their journey back to Ayodhya, their hearts filled with joy and anticipation at the prospect of returning home after years of exile and hardship.

As they traversed through the vast expanse of the kingdom, they were greeted by throngs of well-wishers and adoring citizens who lined the streets to catch a glimpse of their beloved prince and his divine consort. The air was filled with the sound of cheering and celebration, as the people of Ayodhya rejoiced in the return of their beloved prince and the triumph of good over evil.

Upon reaching the outskirts of Ayodhya, Lord Ram, Maa Sita, and Laxman were greeted by King Dasharatha, whose eyes filled with tears of joy at the sight of his beloved son and daughter-in-law. With a heart full of gratitude, he welcomed them back to the kingdom with open arms, his pride and love for them shining brightly in his eyes.

As they made their way through the city streets, Lord Ram and Maa Sita were greeted with scenes of jubilation and festivity, as the citizens of Ayodhya came out in droves to welcome them home. From the youngest child to the oldest elder, everyone rejoiced in the return of their beloved prince and his divine consort, whose valor and righteousness had saved the kingdom from the brink of destruction.

Upon reaching the royal palace, Lord Ram and Maa Sita were greeted by Queen Kaushalya, Queen Kaikeyi, and Queen Sumitra, whose hearts swelled with pride and joy at the sight of their beloved son and daughter-in-law. With tears of happiness streaming down their faces, they embraced Lord Ram and Maa Sita, welcoming them back to the palace with love and affection.

And then, as the sun began to set on the horizon, Lord Ram, Maa Sita, and Laxman made their way to the grand throne room, where King Dasharatha awaited them with his courtiers and advisors. With a sense of solemnity and reverence, they took their places upon the throne, ready to assume their rightful roles as the rulers of Ayodhya once more.

As the people of Ayodhya looked on with admiration and reverence, King Dasharatha addressed the assembled crowd, declaring Lord Ram and Maa Sita as the rightful heirs to the throne of Ayodhya. With tears of pride and happiness in his eyes, he bestowed upon them his blessings and the blessings of the gods, praying for their happiness and prosperity for all eternity.

And as the cheers and applause of the crowd filled the air, Lord Ram and Maa Sita exchanged glances of love and devotion, knowing that their journey was far from over, but that together, they could overcome any obstacle that lay in their path. For theirs was not just a story of triumph and reunion, but a testament to the power of love, courage, and righteousness to overcome even the greatest of challenges.

Part 2: Challenges of Leadership

AS LORD RAM AND MAA Sita settled into their roles as the rulers of Ayodhya, they were faced with a new set of challenges that tested their leadership and resolve. Despite the joyous return to their kingdom, they knew that the responsibilities of governance weighed heavy on their shoulders, and that the task of rebuilding and restoring the kingdom would require all of their skill and determination.

One of the first challenges they faced was the task of reconciling the divisions that had arisen during their absence. In their absence, factions had formed within the kingdom, each vying for power and influence in the wake of the upheaval caused by their exile. Lord Ram and Maa Sita knew that in order to govern effectively, they would need to unite the people of Ayodhya under a common vision and purpose.

To this end, they embarked on a campaign of reconciliation and diplomacy, reaching out to leaders and influencers from all walks of life in an effort to bridge the divides that had arisen during their absence. Through dialogue and compromise, they sought to heal the wounds of the past and forge a path forward that would benefit all citizens of Ayodhya, regardless of their background or beliefs.

Another challenge they faced was the task of rebuilding the kingdom and restoring prosperity to the land. Years of neglect and upheaval had taken their toll on Ayodhya, and Lord Ram and Maa Sita knew that it would take time and effort to undo the damage that had been done. With the help of their advisors and courtiers, they set about implementing a series of reforms and initiatives aimed at revitalizing the economy, improving infrastructure, and promoting social harmony and cohesion.

Yet perhaps the greatest challenge they faced was the task of upholding the principles of dharma and righteousness in the face of adversity and temptation. As rulers, they were faced with countless decisions and dilemmas that tested their moral character and integrity, forcing them to confront difficult choices and make sacrifices for the greater good of the kingdom.

Through it all, Lord Ram and Maa Sita remained steadfast in their commitment to righteousness and justice, their unwavering faith in the divine guiding them through even the darkest of times. Though they faced many trials and tribulations along the way, they emerged stronger and more resilient than ever, their bond of love and devotion serving as a beacon of hope and inspiration for all who looked to them for guidance.

And so, as they faced the challenges of leadership head-on, Lord Ram and Maa Sita remained true to their values and principles, knowing that their ultimate goal was not just to govern, but to create a kingdom where justice, compassion, and righteousness reigned supreme. For theirs was not just a duty, but a sacred calling—a calling to uphold the ideals of dharma and righteousness for the betterment of all beings, for all eternity.

Part 3: Trials of Loyalty

AS LORD RAM AND MAA Sita worked tirelessly to rebuild Ayodhya and uphold the principles of righteousness, they faced a new set of challenges that tested the loyalty and allegiance of those around them. Despite their best efforts to govern with integrity and fairness, they soon discovered that not everyone shared their commitment to dharma and justice.

One of the first signs of trouble came from within their own court, where whispers of dissent and intrigue began to circulate among the nobles and advisors. Some questioned Lord Ram's decisions and leadership, while others openly defied his authority, seeking to undermine his rule and advance their own agendas.

Lord Ram and Maa Sita knew that in order to maintain stability and order within the kingdom, they would need to address these challenges head-on and root out the sources of dissent and treachery. With the help of their loyal allies and advisors, they launched an investigation into the allegations of conspiracy and betrayal, determined to uncover the truth and mete out justice to those responsible.

Their efforts were met with resistance at every turn, as those who sought to undermine their rule went to great lengths to conceal their true intentions and manipulate events to their advantage. Yet, through perseverance and determination, Lord Ram and Maa Sita were able to expose the traitors in their midst and hold them accountable for their actions.

But perhaps the greatest test of loyalty came from within their own family, where tensions and rivalries threatened to tear apart the fabric of their dynasty. Jealousy and ambition reared their ugly heads as rival factions vied for power and influence, their allegiance to Lord Ram and Maa Sita called into question by their own selfish desires.

In the face of these challenges, Lord Ram and Maa Sita remained steadfast in their commitment to justice and righteousness, refusing to compromise their principles or betray the trust of their people. Though the road ahead was fraught with peril and uncertainty, they knew that so long as they stood together, united in their purpose and devotion to each other, they could overcome any obstacle that stood in their way.

And so, as they confronted the trials of loyalty head-on, Lord Ram and Maa Sita emerged stronger and more resilient than ever, their bond of love and devotion serving as a beacon of hope and inspiration for all who looked to them for guidance. For theirs was not just a struggle for power or prestige, but a quest to uphold the principles of righteousness and dharma for the betterment of all beings, for all eternity.

Part 4: The Legacy of Ayodhya

AS LORD RAM AND MAA Sita navigated the trials of leadership and loyalty, their efforts bore fruit in the form of a flourishing and prosperous kingdom. Through their unwavering commitment to righteousness and justice, they were able to restore peace and prosperity to Ayodhya, transforming it into a beacon of hope and inspiration for all who dwelt within its borders.

Under their wise and benevolent rule, the people of Ayodhya experienced a golden age of peace and prosperity, where justice reigned supreme and all beings were treated with dignity and respect. The kingdom thrived under their leadership, with its citizens enjoying abundant harvests, thriving markets, and a sense of security and stability that had long been absent from their lives.

But perhaps the greatest legacy of Lord Ram and Maa Sita's rule was the example they set for future generations to follow. Through their actions and decisions, they demonstrated the importance of integrity, compassion, and selflessness in governance, inspiring others to uphold the principles of righteousness and dharma in their own lives.

Their story became legend, passed down through the ages as a testament to the power of love, courage, and devotion to overcome even the greatest of challenges. In temples and shrines across the land, their images were worshipped and revered, their names spoken with reverence and devotion by all who sought guidance and inspiration.

And though their time upon the throne eventually came to an end, their legacy endured for all eternity, serving as a guiding light for future generations to follow. For in the hearts and minds of the people of Ayodhya, Lord Ram and Maa Sita would forever be remembered as the divine rulers whose love and devotion transformed a kingdom and inspired a nation to greatness.

Chapter 5: The Eternal Love

Part 1: A Bond Beyond Time

AS LORD RAM AND MAA Sita's reign in Ayodhya continued, their love only deepened with each passing day, transcending the boundaries of time and space. Theirs was a love that defied all odds, a bond forged in the fires of adversity and strengthened by the trials they had faced together.

Despite the demands of rulership and the responsibilities that weighed heavily upon them, Lord Ram and Maa Sita always made time for each other, cherishing every moment they spent in each other's company. Whether walking hand in hand through the palace gardens or stealing quiet moments of intimacy amidst the chaos of courtly life, their love remained constant and unwavering.

But even as their love for each other flourished, dark clouds loomed on the horizon, threatening to disrupt the peace and harmony they had worked so hard to achieve. Rumors of unrest and discontent began to spread throughout the kingdom, as whispers of rebellion and betrayal echoed in the halls of power.

Lord Ram and Maa Sita knew that they could not afford to let their guard down, for the forces of darkness were ever vigilant, seeking to exploit any weakness or vulnerability in their defenses. With the help of their loyal allies and advisors, they worked tirelessly to root out the sources of dissent and ensure the safety and security of their kingdom.

Yet amidst the turmoil and uncertainty that surrounded them, Lord Ram and Maa Sita found solace in the knowledge that they faced the challenges together, united in their love and devotion for each other. Their bond remained unbreakable, a beacon of light in the darkest of times, guiding them through the trials and tribulations that lay ahead.

And so, as they faced the uncertain future that lay before them, Lord Ram and Maa Sita took comfort in the knowledge that their love would endure for all eternity, a testament to the power of love to conquer even the greatest of obstacles. For theirs was not just a love story, but a divine union that transcended the boundaries of time and space, binding their souls together for all eternity.

Part 2: Trials of Faith

AS LORD RAM AND MAA Sita's reign continued, their kingdom faced a series of trials that tested the faith and resilience of its people. Amidst the prosperity and peace that they had worked so hard to achieve, new challenges arose that threatened to shake the very foundations of Ayodhya.

One of the first challenges came in the form of a devastating drought that swept across the land, leaving fields barren and crops withered. Despite their best efforts to alleviate the suffering of their people, Lord Ram and Maa Sita knew that they could not single-handedly overcome the forces of nature that threatened to destroy their kingdom.

With the help of their advisors and courtiers, they organized relief efforts and distributed food and supplies to those most in need, but the scale of the disaster was too great for them to overcome alone. As the days turned into weeks and the weeks into months, tensions began to rise within the kingdom, as fear and desperation took hold of the populace.

Amidst the chaos and uncertainty that gripped Ayodhya, Lord Ram and Maa Sita remained steadfast in their faith, trusting in the divine to guide them through the darkest of times. Though the drought tested the resolve of their people, they knew that with patience and perseverance, they would emerge stronger and more united than ever before.

But the challenges facing Ayodhya were far from over, as rumors of war and invasion began to spread throughout the kingdom. Dark forces were gathering on the borders, threatening to engulf the land in conflict and chaos once more.

With tensions escalating and the threat of war looming on the horizon, Lord Ram and Maa Sita knew that they could not afford to hesitate or falter in the face of danger. With the help of their allies and advisors, they mobilized their forces and fortified their defenses, preparing for the inevitable clash that lay ahead.

As the armies of darkness descended upon Ayodhya, Lord Ram and Maa Sita stood united on the battlefield, their hearts filled with courage and determination. With their divine weapons in hand, they fought side by side, leading their troops with valor and honor, their unwavering faith in the righteousness of their cause serving as a beacon of hope for all who fought beside them.

Despite the ferocity of the battle and the overwhelming odds they faced, Lord Ram and Maa Sita emerged victorious, driving back the forces of darkness and securing the safety and security of their kingdom once more. As the cheers of their people echoed through the streets of Ayodhya, they knew that their faith had been rewarded, and that the divine had guided them through yet another trial of faith.

And so, as they stood amidst the ruins of the battlefield, their hearts filled with gratitude and humility, Lord Ram and Maa Sita knew that their love and devotion had triumphed once again, proving that with faith and courage, anything was possible. For theirs was not just a kingdom, but a testament to the power of love, faith, and resilience to overcome even the greatest of challenges, for all eternity.

Part 3: A Divine Revelation

AMIDST THE TRIALS AND tribulations that beset Ayodhya, Lord Ram and Maa Sita found themselves grappling with doubts and uncertainties that tested the very foundations of their faith. Despite their unwavering devotion to each other and to the principles of righteousness, they could not shake the feeling that something was amiss, that a greater challenge lay ahead that would test their resolve like never before.

It was during this time of turmoil and introspection that Lord Ram received a divine revelation, a vision of the future that shook him to his core. In his dreams, he saw a great calamity descending upon Ayodhya, a cataclysmic event that threatened to destroy everything he held dear.

With a heavy heart, Lord Ram confided in Maa Sita about the visions that haunted him, fearing that his divine purpose had been called into question and that their kingdom was doomed to suffer an unimaginable fate. But Maa Sita, ever the embodiment of grace and wisdom, reassured him that together, they would overcome whatever challenges lay ahead, no matter how daunting they may seem.

Determined to uncover the truth behind his visions, Lord Ram embarked on a journey of spiritual enlightenment, seeking guidance from sages and ascetics who dwelt in the remote corners of the kingdom. Through meditation and contemplation, he delved deep into the mysteries of the cosmos, searching for answers to the questions that plagued his mind.

It was during one such meditation that Lord Ram received a revelation from the gods themselves, a message of hope and redemption that filled him with renewed purpose and determination. He learned that the visions he had seen were not a prophecy of doom, but a test of his faith and resolve—a trial that he must endure in order to fulfill his divine destiny and uphold the principles of righteousness and dharma.

With newfound clarity and resolve, Lord Ram returned to Ayodhya, his heart filled with the knowledge that no matter what trials lay ahead, he would face them with courage and conviction, secure in the knowledge that the divine would guide him through even the darkest of times.

And so, as they faced the uncertain future that lay ahead, Lord Ram and Maa Sita did so with a renewed sense of purpose and determination, knowing that their love and devotion would see them through whatever challenges they may encounter. For theirs was not just a journey of kings and queens, but a divine odyssey that would shape the fate of their kingdom and the destiny of all who dwelt within its borders, for all eternity.

Part 4: The Eternal Promise

AS LORD RAM AND MAA Sita continued to navigate the trials and revelations that beset Ayodhya, they were faced with perhaps the greatest challenge of all: the ultimate test of their love and devotion to each other.

Rumors began to spread throughout the kingdom of Ayodhya, whispers of doubt and mistrust that threatened to tear apart the fabric of their divine union. Some questioned the legitimacy of their bond, while others sought to sow discord and dissent among the people, casting doubt upon the purity of their love.

Lord Ram and Maa Sita knew that they could not allow such falsehoods to go unchallenged, for the strength of their love was the foundation upon which their kingdom was built. With unwavering resolve, they confronted their accusers and defended their honor, proclaiming their love for each other to all who would listen.

But even as they fought to preserve their bond, dark forces conspired against them, seeking to undermine their relationship and destroy the unity of their kingdom. In the shadows, unseen and unheard, the seeds of betrayal were sown, threatening to unravel the very fabric of their divine union.

It was during this time of turmoil and uncertainty that Maa Sita made a solemn vow to Lord Ram, a promise that would echo through the ages and endure for all eternity. With tears in her eyes and love in her heart, she swore to stand by his side through thick and thin, to weather whatever storms may come their way, and to never waver in her love and devotion for him, no matter what challenges they may face.

Touched by her words and overwhelmed by emotion, Lord Ram pledged to honor her vow and to cherish their love for all eternity. With a heart full of gratitude and love, he vowed to protect her with his life and to uphold the sanctity of their bond, no matter what trials may lie ahead.

And so, as they stood together, united in their love and devotion, Lord Ram and Maa Sita knew that no matter what challenges they may face, their bond would remain unbreakable, their love eternal. For theirs was not just a promise, but a divine covenant—a testament to the power of love to conquer even the greatest of obstacles, and to endure for all eternity.

Poem;

In the saga of love divine,
Lord Ram and Sita's story does shine,
A tale of devotion, pure and true,
In hearts of many, forever ensue.
In the forests deep, they roamed,
Their love, like stars, brightly foamed,
Through trials and tests, they stood strong,
Their bond, a melody, an eternal song.
With each glance, a world did unfold,
In their love, stories of old retold,
In Sita's eyes, Ram found his peace,
Their love, a bond that would never cease.
Together they faced the darkest of night,
Their love, a beacon, shining bright,
In each other's arms, they found solace,
Their love, a sanctuary, a sacred palace.
In the heart of Ayodhya, their love did bloom,
Their bond, a fragrance, filling every room,
Through every trial, their love did grow,
A testament to the depths of love's glow.
So let us raise our voices high,
In praise of love that never shall die,
For in the love of Ram and Sita divine,
Eternal truth and beauty we shall find.

Conclusion: The Eternal Legacy
In the annals of time, there exists a tale,
Of love and devotion that will never pale,
The story of Lord Ram and Maa Sita's bond,
A saga of love, eternally fond.
Through trials and tribulations, they did tread,
Their love, a flame that never fled,
In the heart of Ayodhya, their kingdom grand,
They ruled with justice, hand in hand.
Their journey was not without its share of strife,
But in each other's love, they found life,
Together they faced the darkest of night,
Their love, a beacon, shining bright.
And though their time upon this earth may end,
Their legacy lives on, a message to send,
Of the power of love to conquer all,
And the importance of standing tall.
So let us remember the love they shared,
A bond that nothing could ever tear,
For in their story, we find our own,
A testament to the love that has grown.
And as we close the chapter on their tale,
Let us remember, without fail,
That in the love of Lord Ram and Maa Sita true,
We find the strength to see us through.

Gratitude and Apology

Dear Readers,

As we come to the end of this journey through the divine love story of Lord Ram and Maa Sita, I would like to express my heartfelt gratitude to each and every one of you who has accompanied me on this adventure.

Your support and encouragement have meant the world to me, and I am truly humbled by the love and kindness you have shown. It has been an honor and a privilege to share this timeless tale with you, and I hope that it has touched your hearts as deeply as it has touched mine.

However, before we part ways, I would like to take a moment to offer my sincere apologies if, in the course of recounting this sacred story, I have inadvertently made any errors or caused any offense. It was never my intention to disrespect the divine figures of Lord Ram and Maa Sita, or to portray their story in a manner that could be deemed inappropriate or disrespectful.

If at any point my words have fallen short of the reverence and respect that Lord Ram and Maa Sita deserve, I humbly ask for your forgiveness. My only aim in sharing their story was to celebrate the eternal love and devotion that they shared, and to honor the timeless wisdom and teachings that their lives exemplify.

Once again, I extend my deepest gratitude to each and every one of you for joining me on this journey. May the love and blessings of Lord Ram and Maa Sita be with you always.

With heartfelt thanks and warmest regards,

Mrigendra Bharti

Founder at Mrigendra Bharti Group and Sellbrochure Vymish Entertainment

About the Author

Mrigendra Bharti, born on June 29, 2004, in South Delhi, India, is a multifaceted individual recognized as the owner of Mrigendra Bharti Group InfoTech India Co. Pvt Ltd. Beyond his entrepreneurial endeavors, he is a distinguished music producer, director, and a budding writer.

Embarking on his professional journey at a young age, Mrigendra Bharti's visionary leadership has led to the establishment of several successful ventures, including Croma Music Series Entertainment, Sellbrochure, Fauget Innovative, and more.

What sets Mrigendra apart is his early initiation into the world of business. His foray into the unknown realms of entrepreneurship began during his 10th-grade years, where he delved into the music industry. This initial venture laid the foundation for subsequent achievements, showcasing his dedication and resilience.

Having honed his skills in music, Mrigendra Bharti not only demonstrated significant growth in his craft but also expanded his professional network. His passion extends beyond music, encompassing app and website development, as well as graphic design.

Fueled by his creative aspirations, Mrigendra established the Mrigendra Bharti Group, a company specializing in website and app development. Currently, he collaborates with a dedicated team, collectively working on ambitious projects that promise innovation and excellence.

Mrigendra's journey serves as an inspiration, particularly for today's students, highlighting the potential of youthful determination and the ability to transform innovative ideas into successful businesses. As he continues to make strides in various domains, Mrigendra Bharti remains a dynamic force, contributing vibrancy to the realms of business, music, and technology.

Read more at https://www.imwriter-mrigendra.rf.gd.